Play Fair!

Kelly Doudna

Consulting Editor, Diane Craig, M.A./Reading Specialist

Published by ABDO Publishing Company, 4940 Viking Drive, Edina, Minnesota 55435.

Copyright © 2007 by Abdo Consulting Group, Inc. International copyrights reserved in all countries. No part of this book may be reproduced in any form without written permission from the publisher. SandCastle™ is a trademark and logo of ABDO Publishing Company.

Printed in the United States.

Credits
Edited by: Pam Price
Curriculum Coordinator: Nancy Tuminelly
Cover and Interior Design and Production: Mighty Media
Photo Credits: AbleStock, Brand X Pictures, Hemera, ShutterStock

Library of Congress Cataloging-in-Publication Data

Doudna, Kelly, 1963-
　Play fair! / Kelly Doudna.
　　p. cm. -- (Character concepts)
　ISBN-13: 978-1-59928-739-3
　ISBN-10: 1-59928-739-0
　1. Sportsmanship--Juvenile literature. I. Title.

GV706.3.D68 2007
175--dc22

2006032280

SandCastle™ books are created by a professional team of educators, reading specialists, and content developers around five essential components—phonemic awareness, phonics, vocabulary, text comprehension, and fluency—to assist young readers as they develop reading skills and strategies and increase their general knowledge. All books are written, reviewed, and leveled for guided reading, early reading intervention, and Accelerated Reader® programs for use in shared, guided, and independent reading and writing activities to support a balanced approach to literacy instruction.

Let Us Know

SandCastle would like to hear your stories about reading this book. What is your favorite page? Was there something hard that you needed help with? Share the ups and downs of learning to read. We want to hear from you! To get posted on the ABDO Publishing Company Web site, send us e-mail at:

sandcastle@abdopublishing.com

SandCastle Level: Transitional

Character Concept
Play Fair!

Your character is a part of who you are. It is how you act when you go somewhere. It is how you get along with other people. It is even what you do when no one is looking!

You show character by playing fair. You have good sportsmanship. You don't cheat. You never make fun of a player on the losing team!

Mia learns how to golf. She doesn't play well at first. But she keeps a positive attitude. Mia has good sportsmanship.

Jennifer and her teammates listen to their coach. They know it takes a team effort to win. They play with good sportsmanship.

Lucy sits out for a while. She gives another girl a chance to go into the game. Lucy plays fair.

Sam's team won the game. Sam tells Michael that his team played well too. Sam has good sportsmanship.

Dylan scored his first basket. Dylan's mother is proud, but she's even more proud that he plays fair.

Claire plays baseball
with good sportsmanship.
It helps her team do better,
and Claire thinks that's hip.

Sometimes Claire
plays in the game.
Sometimes she sits out.
If things don't
go her way,
she knows she
shouldn't pout.

Claire doesn't make a big show when she scores a run. She knows that her teammates helped get the job done.

Whether the team
has lost or won,
it doesn't bother Claire.
The game is done,
and she knows that
they've all played fair!

Did You Know?

The US Youth Soccer Organization has more than three million registered members.

The high five was in wide use by the late 1970s. Both a college basketball player and a major league baseball player claim to have invented it.

The Olympics gives a special medal to reward athletes who show good sportsmanship. The first one was awarded in 1964 to an Italian bobsled racer who helped one of his competitors.

Glossary

attitude – the way you think or feel about something.

effort – the work it takes to do something.

fair – according to the rules.

hip – cool or trendy.

positive – being upbeat and expecting a good outcome.

pout – to show unhappiness by pushing out the lips.

sportsmanship – the good attitude and behavior, such as fair play and respect, shown by an athlete.

About SandCastle™

A professional team of educators, reading specialists, and content developers created the SandCastle™ series to support young readers as they develop reading skills and strategies and increase their general knowledge. The SandCastle™ series has four levels that correspond to early literacy development in young children. The levels are provided to help teachers and parents select appropriate books for young readers.

Emerging Readers
(no flags)

Beginning Readers
(1 flag)

Transitional Readers
(2 flags)

Fluent Readers
(3 flags)

These levels are meant only as a guide. All levels are subject to change.

To see a complete list of SandCastle™ books and other nonfiction titles from ABDO Publishing Company, visit **www.abdopublishing.com** or contact us at:
4940 Viking Drive, Edina, Minnesota 55435 • 1-800-800-1312 • fax: 1-952-831-1632